Race to the Tower of Power

adapted by Catherine Lukas
based on the original teleplay by Adam Peltzman
illustrated by Dave Aikins

SIMON SPOTLIGHT/NICK JR.
New York   London   Toronto   Sydney

Based on the TV series *Nick Jr. The Backyardigans*™ as seen on Nick Jr.®

 SIMON SPOTLIGHT
An imprint of Simon & Schuster Children's Publishing Division
1230 Avenue of the Americas, New York, New York 10020
© 2006 Viacom International Inc. All rights reserved. NICK JR.,
Nick Jr. The Backyardigans, and all related titles, logos, and characters
are trademarks of Viacom International Inc. All rights reserved, including
the right of reproduction in whole or in part in any form.
SIMON SPOTLIGHT and colophon are registered trademarks of Simon & Schuster, Inc.
Manufactured in the United States of America
10 9 8 7 6 5 4 3
ISBN-13: 978-1-4169-0799-2
ISBN-10: 1-4169-0799-8

Pablo and Tyrone were playing in the backyard.

"Wa-ha-haa! We're supervillains!" said Pablo. "I'm Yucky Man. I have the power to make things yucky!"

"And I'm Dr. Shrinky!" said Tyrone. "I have the power to make things small! Wa-ha-haa!"

"Hey, Dr. Shrinky!" said Pablo. "Let's use our supervillain powers to take over the world!"

"Yeah!" replied Tyrone. "To do that, we need to capture the Key to the World that's hidden in the Tower of Power! Wa-ha-haa! Let's go!"

As soon as the villains left, two superheroes bounded into the yard.

"I'm Captain Hammer!" said Austin proudly. "I can build anything!"

"And I'm Weather Woman!" announced Uniqua. "I have the power to change the weather!"

"Look!" said Austin, pointing to a tiny, gooey slide. "The supervillains have been here!"

"They must be after the Key to the World," said Uniqua. "Come on. It's superheroes to the rescue!"

Meanwhile, Pablo and Tyrone were making villainous plans in the Forest of Darkness. . . .

"This way, Yucky Man!" said Tyrone. "We need to cross the Land of Cold!"

"Not so fast, supervillains," said a voice.
"Superheroes!" yelled Pablo.
The heroes chased after the villains.
"Ground . . . get sticky!" ordered Pablo.
ZLURP! The ground beneath the superheroes turned into a yucky, smelly mud pit.

"We're stuck!" cried Uniqua as she watched the villains escape. "Quick! Captain Hammer—get us out of here!"

Austin found a stone and banged it with his superhero hammer. Quick as a flash, a mud-sucking vacuum cleaner appeared and sucked up all the yucky mud.

"Come on!" called Uniqua. "We can't let the villains get to the Tower of Power before we do!"

"Brrr!" said Austin a few moments later. "I guess we've reached the Land of Cold."

"Look!" said Uniqua, pointing. The villains were sliding across the ice toward the Tower. "Quick! Build us a boat, Captain Hammer!"

BANG! Austin hit a twig with his toy hammer. . . .

And—POOF!—a boat appeared.

"And now I'll use my superpowers to change the weather!" said Uniqua. "Weather change—to hot!"

The sun grew hot. CRACK! The ice began to melt.

"Uh-oh!" said Tyrone. "The ice is melting!"

Moments later the two villains stood stranded on a tiny iceberg while the superheroes rowed past them.

Then Pablo had an idea. He pointed at the water.

"Superheroes hate yucky, smelly goo," he said. "Water—turn to gobbly-goo!"

ZLURF!

"Eeew!" said Uniqua. "I hate yucky goo!"
"You can't defeat the power of yuck!" Pablo shouted as the supervillains sloshed past.

"I know!" said Austin. "I'll build a bridge!" WHACK! went his hammer. Moments later the superheroes were running over a bridge and toward the Tower of Power.

"Drat!" said Pablo as the superheroes dashed past them. "Foiled again! Do something, Dr. Shrinky!"

Tyrone pointed at Austin and unleashed his shrinking rays. ZAP!

"We've got to get to the top first!" squeaked a tiny Austin as the villains ran into the Tower. "It's up to you, Weather Woman!"

Uniqua waved her arms. WHOOSH! A twister picked them up off the ground and carried them up, up, up to the top of the tower.

"At last!" said Pablo. "We've got the Key to the World!"
"Oh, no you don't!" shouted Uniqua.
As Tyrone and Pablo shot their rays at Uniqua, she grabbed the key and held it up. . . .

The rays bounced off the key and back onto the villains, shrinking them and covering them with goo. Then Austin banged a paper clip with his hammer. The tiny, gooey villains found themselves trapped in a cage.

"Please let us out!" said Pablo. "We promise to be nice!"

"If we let you out," said Uniqua, "then you have to promise to be superheroes. And instead of stealing the Key to the World, promise that you'll help us protect it."

"We promise!" said Pablo and Tyrone.
Austin opened the door to the cage, and out they came.
Then Tyrone made all three of them big again.

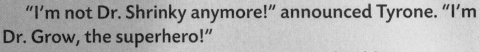

"I'm not Dr. Shrinky anymore!" announced Tyrone. "I'm Dr. Grow, the superhero!"

"And I'm now . . . Very Clean Guy!" said Pablo. Suddenly they heard a rumbling sound.

"I'm also a very *hungry* guy," Pablo said, laughing.

"Let's all go to my house for a supersnack," suggested Austin. "We have granola bars."

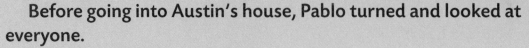

Before going into Austin's house, Pablo turned and looked at everyone.

"Wa-ha-haa!" he cackled. Uniqua looked at him sternly.

"Oops!" said Pablo. "I mean . . . superheroes to the rescue!"